Dinosaur on Passover

Dinosaur on Passover

Diane Levin Rauchwerger

pictures by Jason Wolff

KAR-BEN
PUBLISHING

There's a dino knocking on my door
'Cause PASSOVER is near.
He wants to sweep the chametz* out—
He's in the way I fear.

* Bread, cookies, and other foods not eaten on Passover

He grates a hunk of horseradish
Cries buckets full of tears
When I tell him how the Hebrews slaved
For Pharaoh all those years.

We want to start the seder
But Dino can't be found.
He's in the pantry juggling
Matzah boxes all around.

He helps me sing the questions
He knows that there are four.
Tonight, why is there matzah
And bitter herbs we call maror?

Why do we dip our veggies twice
And why do we recline?
And Dino also wants to know
When he can drink his wine.

When Dino hears how Moses begged
to "Let My People Go,"
He stomps his feet like Pharaoh
Yelling, "No, No, No, No, No!"

We tell how Pharaoh suffered,
God was angry as can be,
Sending hail and darkness, frogs and bugs
'Til Pharaoh said, "Go free!"

Dino munches on the matzah,
Dips his pinky in his cup,
Lets drops of wine fall everywhere
And tries to wipe them up.

He searches for the afikomen
The books fly left and right.
I have to help him find it
So it doesn't take all night.

He runs to open up the door
To see Elijah there,
But when the neighbor's dog runs in
It gives us quite a scare.

Before the seder's over
Dino's curled up in a heap.
We'll have to end without him
'Cause he's fallen fast asleep.

The spring festival of **Passover** (*Pesach* in Hebrew) celebrates the Biblical story of the exodus of the Jewish slaves from Egypt. To prepare for the holiday, families clean their homes to remove all the *chametz* — bread and other foods not allowed to be eaten during the holiday. The holiday begins with a *seder*, a ritual meal during which the story of Passover is recited and symbolic foods are eaten. These include *matzah*, unleavened bread that recalls the haste with which the Jews left Egypt, and *maror*, a bitter herb that symbolizes the bitterness of slavery under Pharaoh. It is said that the prophet Elijah visits every seder to bring the blessing of peace.

KAR-BEN PUBLISHING, INC.
A division of Lerner Publishing Group
241 First Avenue North
Minneapolis, MN 55401 U.S.A.
800-4KARBEN

Website address: www.karben.com

Library of Congress Cataloging-in-Publication Data

Rauchwerger, Diane Levin.
    Dinosaur on Passover / by Diane Levin Rauchwerger ; illustrations by Jason Wolff.
       p. cm.
    Summary: An enthusiastic dinosaur comes to a young boy's house to join him in celebrating Passover.
     ISBN: 1—58013—156—5 (lib. bdg. : alk. paper)
    [1. Passover—Fiction. 2. Seder—Fiction. 3. Dinosaurs—Fiction.] I. Wolff, Jason, ill. II. Title.
PZ7.R1953Din 2006
[E]—dc22   2005003702

Manufactured in the United States of America
1 2 3 4 5 6 – JR – 11 10 09 08 07 06